P9-EJJ-273

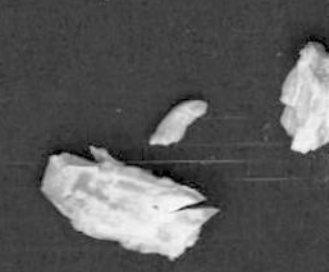

A Proper Little Lady

by NETTE HILTON

Illustrated by CATHY WILCOX

ORCHARD BOOKS • NEW YORK

First American Edition 1990 published by Orchard Books
First published in Australia by William Collins Pty Ltd

Orchard Books, A division of Franklin Watts, Inc.
387 Park Avenue South, New York, NY 10016

Manufactured in the United States of America. Printed by General Offset, Co., Inc. Bound by Horowitz/Rae. The text of this book is set in 16 pt. New Aster. The illustrations are pen and ink and watercolors, reproduced in four colors. Book design by Mina Greenstein
1 3 5 7 9 10 8 6 4 2

Library of Congress Cataloging-in-Publication Data
Hilton, Nette. A proper little lady / by Nette Hilton ; illustrated by Cathy Wilcox.—1st American ed. p. cm. Summary: Annabella feels like a proper little lady in her fancy clothes but finds them a bit inconvenient when she goes out and gets embroiled in messy fun.
ISBN 0-531-05860-3.—ISBN 0-531-08460-4 (lib. bdg.)
[1. Clothing and dress—Fiction. 2. Behavior—Fiction.] I. Wilcox, Cathy, ill. II. Title.
PZ7.H56775Pr 1990 [E]—dc20 89-35399 CIP AC

One day, Annabella Jones looked in the mirror and decided that she would be a proper little lady.

First she put on her pale blue dress
with the big white bow.

Then she put on a frilly white petticoat
and her second-best pair of navy-blue knickers.

She turned this way and that.

Swish, swish, swish went the pale blue dress.

Then she put on her lacy pink socks
with the tiny blue frill
and her shiny black shoes.

She turned this way and that.
Swish, swish, swish went the pale blue dress.
Tap, tap, tap went the shiny black shoes.

Then she reached to the top shelf of her closet
and took down her big straw hat
and a pair of white lace gloves.

She put them on and turned this way and that.
Swish, swish, swish went the pale blue dress.
Tap, tap, tap went the shiny black shoes.

"Mmmmm," said Annabella. "What next?"
And she looked under the bed and found her
box marked "Special junk." She pulled out a long
gold chain and draped it around her neck.

She turned this way and that.
Swish, swish, swish went the pale blue dress.
Tap, tap, tap went the shiny black shoes.
Chink, chink, chink went the long gold chain.
"There," said Annabella.

“My,” said Mrs. Jones as she pushed a daisy back into place. “You look like a proper little lady.”

"Thank you," said Annabella. "I certainly do."
And Annabella did.

Annabella Jones walked down the street.
Swish, swish, swish went the pale blue dress.
Tap, tap, tap went the shiny black shoes.
Chink, chink, chink went the long gold chain.

"Annabella! Annabella Jones!" called Mrs. Mison. "Byron has chased Merriwether up the mulberry tree. Can you get him down?"

"Of course," said Annabella in her most polite voice. "I would be delighted."

But first she carefully removed her white lace gloves, her shiny black shoes, and her big straw hat, and tucked her pale blue dress into her second-best pair of navy-blue knickers.

Swish, swish, swish went the pale blue dress.
Tap, tap, tap went the shiny black shoes.
Chink, chink, chink went the long gold chain.

"Annabella! Annabella Jones!" yelled the Murphy twins. "Come and show us how to ride this go-cart down the hill."

“Of course,” said Annabella in a rather loud ladylike voice. “Just a minute.” And she removed her white lace gloves, her shiny black shoes, and her big straw hat.

But she forgot to tuck her pale blue dress into her second-best pair of navy-blue knickers.

ZZZooomm
ZZooomm
Zoom
BOWEN
TOMATOES

Flop, flop, flop went the pale blue dress.
Tap, tap, tap went the shiny black shoes.
Chink, chink, chink went the long gold chain.

"Annabella! Annabella Jones!" yelled the Ogdens.
"Come play ball. You can be on Christopher's team!"

"Hold on!" shouted Annabella. And she took off her white lace gloves and shoved them into her pocket.

Flop. Flop. Flop went the pale blue dress.
Clunk. Clunk. Clunk went the dirty black shoes.
Snap. Snap. Snap went the broken gold chain.

"Oh dear, oh dear," said Mrs. Jones.

"Perhaps it would be easier to be a proper little lady if you wore these the next time."

And Annabella did just that.